THE TIME TRAVELER'S ADVENTURE

ADRIANNA WARD

Book Cover by Kim Ward
Edited by: Kim Ward

Published by GWN Publishing, LLC | www.gwnpublishing.com

ISBN: 978-1-965971-07-9

I dedicate this book to my mom, my dad, my teachers, my good friends, and anyone who helped me and promised they would read it when it was published.

Thank you mom and dad for helping me with this and always supporting me.

A Note From the Author

Hi, welcome to *The Time Traveler's Adventure!* If you're reading this book right now, it was made by a young author, so if you'd like to offer feedback, that would be amazing!

First, I will introduce the characters. The main character's name (me): Caroline Bella Lee. Mom's name: Andrea Kella Lee. Dad's name: Bryon Kane Lee. Random friend's name: Luca Andrea Watson. Now that I've gone over the characters and their names, the setting will be Cumberland High School of Magic. Since I've covered everything to start out with, let's get on with the story!

Also, this is my first book, so please don't judge too hard. There will this is my first book so please don't judge too hard, and there will be more characters, those are just main!

Contents

1. The Beginning — 1

2. Glad We Were Safe — 5

3. Exploring the School and its Classes — 9

4. The Trouble Starts — 13

5. Bendy and Being Famous — 19

6. The Adventure Comes to an End — 21

7. A Few Years Later We Go Back — 25

Afterword — 29

Acknowledgements — 31

About the Author — 33

CHAPTER ONE

The Beginning

Just like any ordinary day, I, Caroline Bella Lee, was bored—it was summer vacation. I had just finished my chores, and my parents were outside, so I went to my room. Then, the front door opened, and my parents, Bryon Kane Lee and Andrea Kella Lee, walked in with happy-ish expressions.

They smiled and said, "Caroline Lee, your friend Luca's parents called and said she wants you to come over for a week-long sleepover!"

My face lit up with excitement—I love my friend! I responded, "Really!? Yes! Yes! Yes! I'd love to! Let me pack my things right now!"

I grabbed my bag, threw it on my bed, and started packing. I added more than just clothes.

Now, you might say, "*Yeah, you should add more than clothes, like a book or some toys,*" but I hate to break it to you—this isn't just any ordinary friend.

My parents think it's just a regular sleepover with the same friend, but Luca is different. She's incredibly smart, and every time I go over, it turns into a new adventure.

My mom said, "We're going to let you pack. We're going out for dinner, so be safe."

I replied, "Yeah, of course! It's not like we're gonna go swimming with dolphins or anything!"

My parents gave me a look but didn't say anything. After they left, I grabbed my cell phone and called Luca.

"Hey! Are you packing?" she asked.

"Yes," I replied.

"Good! Now, I know your parents, and I know for a fact they're out of the house. It's not rare for them to do that, so—" As she flipped her camera, I saw something awesome and definitely *not* human-like.

I gasped. "A TIME MACHINE! OH MY GOSH, YOU'RE AMAZING!"

I repeated, "You're amazing," at least ten times—I was in complete shock! My friend laughed as she tried to recover from her laughter.

"Yeah, yeah. I'm not surprised I made this. Now, I was reading and found out that in the future, there will be magic and a magical school, so I want to travel there and see if we get magical powers. *Oh, also—get here by 10:00 PM sharp!*"

I agreed and said, "Yeah, I just finished packing. I'm coming over now, but there's a problem... I don't have anything to ride, and your house is like an hour away."

She laughed. "Looks like you're walking! Yeah, good luck. I'll be waiting outside on my bike or playing basketball."

I sighed, threw my bag over my shoulder, and started walking.

Before I took my first step, I thought, *Well, this isn't gonna get done by itself.* So I started my journey.

An hour later, it was 6:00 PM—she had left at 5:00 PM. As soon as I saw her house, I yelled, "LUCA WATSON, I'M HERE! I'M HERE! IT'S A MIRACLE!"

I ran toward her. She burst out laughing at what I said, but I didn't care—she's my best friend.

CHAPTER TWO

Glad We Were Safe

As we stepped into the time machine, my friend looked at me nervously and said, "Caroline Bella... I-I-I messed up. I forgot what I had it set on..."

I looked at her and said, "We'll pray that it's a safe o—"

Before I could finish, we teleported. We both anxiously stepped out. Safe to say, we had only traveled to our neighbor's house—just two days into the future. We laughed it off, relieved that it wasn't anything worse. After shaking off the nerves, we went back into the time machine. This time, Luca made sure to fix it before we took off for the school.

A few minutes later, the machine finished teleporting us. We stepped out, but to our surprise, it wasn't as amazing as we had imagined.

Luca sighed. "It sounded way more exciting in the books. I think books just exaggerate too much—*way too much*."

I nodded in agreement. "Welp, the adventure isn't gonna get more interesting than this. And we have no choice but to stay because the time machine disappeared."

Luca turned around, and when she saw that it had truly vanished, she froze in fear. I reassured her, and with no other option, we decided to move forward.

As we walked into the building, a teacher spotted us.

"Oh! New students! Welcome. Follow me, and I'll get you checked in!" he said.

We followed him and got registered. As we made our way through the halls, we noticed things were interesting. The pictures on the walls moved, magic randomly sparked to life even though we were the only ones in the hallway, and there were no lights anywhere.

I frowned. "No lights, moving pictures, and magic happening on its own? I don't think this is a certified place. And from what I see, I think you need magic to navigate this school. I don't even know if we have magic!"

We found our classroom and walked in. The students and the teacher smiled at us.

The teacher introduced herself, "Hi, you can call me Barbra Kendall. Take a seat, and we will see if you have magic—and if so, what type of magic. If you don't, then you will be expelled from the school."

I nodded. "Okay, madam."

Luca, much less enthusiastic, muttered, "Okay... just make it quick."

I turned to her and whispered, "You're the one who wanted to go on this trip, and now we're stuck here! It's all your fault, so don't come crying or complaining!"

She gave me a small nod, and soon after, we discovered that we did have magic. My abilities were water and wind, while Luca's were fire and water.

To be honest, I have no idea how she got fire and water—those two don't even go together! It hurts my brain just thinking about it.

The next morning, we woke up, got dressed, and headed to breakfast. During breakfast, we received mail—delivered by invisible staff. It was kind of cool (and creepy) to see envelopes floating through the air before dropping onto the tables.

I opened mine and read:

Hi Caroline Bella Lee, I hope you have a great time. There will be flying classes after breakfast in the courtyard, followed by lunch and free time. Oh, also—if you want to get a pet, there will be a pet shop in the courtyard. Have a great time, and do not use forbidden spells.

That was all it said.

I turned to Luca. "What does yours say?"

She glanced at hers and replied, "Same thing—just with my name instead of yours."

CHAPTER THREE

Exploring the School and its Classes

After class, we heard the bell ring, so we got up. The teacher left, and the students stayed behind, chatting and laughing. Luca Watson and I, however, stayed quiet the whole time—we just wanted to take in our surroundings.

Luca turned to me and said, "Hey, let's split up and explore."

I nodded. "Yeah, we should! Bye, see you later!"

So we split up. As I walked, I saw the most amazing things. It was nighttime, and the paths were beautifully lit by the moonlight. When I looked up, the sky was filled with countless stars—it felt so nostalgic. I loved this place.

At some point, I stopped at a pet shop and decided to buy a pet—a coyote cub. After purchasing it, I picked it up and continued exploring. The forest paths were glowing softly with torches, making the darkness even more magical. Since it was nighttime, the entire atmosphere felt *ten times* better.

I walked a bit more, observing students who were either studying, playing games, or feeding and caring for their pets. It was the best feeling. There was even a campsite where students could hang out, eat, or cook food over an open fire—roasting marshmallows and making s'mores. The air was filled with laughter, mostly from silly dad jokes being told around the campfire. The energy there was incredible—welcoming, humble, and strong.

Then, the principal's voice echoed through the air, "All students, go to your dorms and get rest. All students, go to your dorms and get rest."

With my coyote cub in hand, I wrapped it in my jacket to keep it warm as I made my way back to the dorm.

When I arrived, I saw Luca Watson and greeted her excitedly. "Hey, how are you?! Before you ask, I'm good! It was such a cool place, and also—I got a coyote pup!"

She smiled. "I'm doing good! I'm glad you're doing good, too. That's awesome because there are crates, food, and water for the animals in the dorm. Oh, and I stocked us up on food and made our beds!"

I grinned. "Thanks! That's all great to hear! I'm going to put—" I suddenly stopped mid-sentence. "Wait... I forgot! We need to name the coyote! What should we name her?"

We thought for a while before Luca snapped her fingers. "How about... Bendy?"

I gasped. "That's an awesome name!"

I smiled and continued, "Now, as I was saying—I'm going to put Bendy in her crate, get ready for bed, and then sleep. So, good night!"

Luca nodded. "Okay! Me too. Good night and sweet dreams."

I nodded back, got ready, placed Bendy in her crate, and went to sleep.

The next morning, I yawned and sat up in bed. Luca Watson was still sleeping, so I made sure to be quiet. I checked on Bendy—she was still fast asleep. I chuckled softly, carefully opened her cage, and got ready for the day.

Later, before class started, Luca walked in, and we began the lesson. That day, we learned about how to control our magic.

That night, a dance—kind of like prom—was being held, so Luca and I decided to go.

"I love these songs! And I *love* your dress!" I said to her excitedly. "I bought mine!"

I laughed, and she did too.

"Thank you! And you look nice too," she replied with a smile.

In the middle of the prom, just as everyone was having fun, the music suddenly stopped. Silence filled the room.

Then, someone screamed, "EVERYONE, DON'T SAY A WORD—LOOK UP!"

We all did.

Suddenly, the song *Celestial* by Ed Sheeran started playing, and right above us, a meteor shower filled the sky!

It was breathtaking. A *perfect* memory.

Chapter Four

The Trouble Starts

The next day, Luca Watson and I were wandering the halls when two boys approached us.

One of them smirked and said, "Oh look, two girls all by themselves. Wonder if they can fight back!"

The other boy suddenly pretended to be hurt—he was good at it. His friend gasped in *fake* shock and ran to get a teacher.

I exchanged an annoyed glance with Luca, who looked completely offended.

The teacher arrived and, without hesitation, believed the boys. We tried explaining, but the teacher wouldn't listen. The boys walked away, snickering to themselves, while we got sent to detention—by the principal—for an hour. *A whole hour*!

As we sat there, I turned to Luca and whispered, "We need to show those boys they can't mess with us."

She grinned mischievously. "How about we prank them? We'll do exactly what they did to us—but this time, we'll make sure they end up in detention writing sentences."

I chuckled and nodded in agreement.

That night, back at our dorms, I played with Bendy before going to bed.

The next day, Luca and I put our plan into action. We both faked being hurt, just like the boys had done, and—just like before—the teacher believed us without question. We walked away laughing, victorious.

Unfortunately for the boys... they weren't as lucky.

Instead of just writing sentences in detention, they were given *paragraphs*! That wasn't part of the plan—we only meant for them to write a few lines! We didn't find out about their punishment until lunchtime, when the boys approached us, looking exhausted.

"Okay, okay, we're sorry," one of them muttered.

"We *really* shouldn't have done that to you," the other one admitted.

Luca and I exchanged looks, then nodded. "Apology accepted."

With that settled, we finished our lunch and decided to explore the forest.

As we walked along the trails, I took in the surroundings and sighed happily. "I love this forest. It's so peaceful—the birds chirping, the wind howling through the trees, and the woodpeckers pecking. It's the calmest place here."

Luca nodded in agreement. "Yeah, I love the vibe. Everything here has been a good vibe so far."

Bendy trotted alongside us, his tail wagging as we enjoyed the quiet. But the peacefulness didn't last long.

The sun set quickly, and before we knew it, darkness had settled in. Suddenly, Bendy let out a low growl, his fur standing on end. Luca and I froze, instantly on high alert. Before we could react, Bendy lunged forward, attacking *something—or someone* and a loud scream cut through the air.

"GET OFF! GET OFF!" a voice yelled in panic.

My heart pounded. "BENDY, COME HERE! NOW!" I shouted.

To my surprise, Bendy happily trotted back, his tail wagging as if nothing had happened. I quickly grabbed a torch and lit it, illuminating the scene in front of us.

To our horror... it was the security guard—and some of his friends.

My face turned red with shame. "Oh no... I'm so sorry! *So, so sorry!*"

Luca looked just as shocked as I felt.

The guards, still recovering, gave us a stern look. "You better keep that animal under control, young lady," one of them scolded.

I crossed my arms. "It's a *coyote*, thank you very much! And I *just* got him. His name is Bendy, and he was just being protective!"

The other guards turned to the main security officer, who had been the one Bendy had attacked. He was completely speechless at my quick comeback—especially coming from someone as young as me.

With nothing else to say, I grabbed Bendy's leash, and Luca and I made our way back to the dorm. Once inside, I put Bendy in his crate, and we both got ready for bed.

"Good night, Luca Watson!" I said sleepily.

"Good night, Caroline Lee!" she replied.

The next morning, surprisingly... nothing happened. It was just a normal, ordinary day. And honestly? I was kind of glad. Well... nothing major happened, at least.

CHAPTER FIVE

Bendy and Being Famous

A month had passed, and Bendy had grown even more. His fur was now a beautiful mix of gray and white, and everyone adored him. I took him everywhere with me and Luca Watson—he was practically part of our duo.

One morning, as Luca and I got ready for the day, I joked, "We should get Bendy his own costume—like, make him famous or something!"

Luca laughed. "We *should*!"

I blinked, a little shocked by her response. "Wait... I was *joking*—but okay! Let's do it!"

So, after getting ready, we brought Bendy to the pet store. For some reason, our school had a pet shop, which I always thought was *cool-but-weird*.

As soon as we walked in, people started complimenting Bendy left and right. He even got treats from random people! It turned out he was already well-known at the pet shop, too. The staff loved him, and he got more treats than anything else. He was one happy boy.

We picked out the perfect costume for him—a tiny doggy tuxedo, a fake gold pair of glasses, and a necklace that said *FAMOUS*.

When we got back to school, everyone loved it. Even the teachers laughed! Turns out, the school *does* have a sense of humor after all!

CHAPTER SIX

The Adventure Comes to an End

A year had passed. Bendy, Luca Watson, and I had all grown up. Bendy was now a bit older than an adult coyote, I was 16, and Luca was 14.

A long time ago, we had texted our parents, letting them know we were on an adventure. Their response?

"Cool! Have fun. Take as long as you want."

So, I figured, *Surely they're okay with us taking this long...*

Well... yeah, about that.

Yesterday, out of nowhere, they texted, "You're old enough now. You and your friend should start going off on your own."

So, I guess we were officially old enough to be independent.

One day, after taking Bendy on a walk, I returned to find Luca Watson packing her bags.

Confused, I asked, "Luca Watson... are we *leaving?*"

She nodded. "Yeah, we are. This whole journey was just to see if magic was real and all that stuff."

I pouted. "Aww, okay. But can we at least explore the areas we haven't been to yet?"

She smiled. "Yes! That was part of my plan, too."

I grinned. "Okay, let's go!"

"But first," she reminded me, "we need to pack—and pack some stuff for Bendy, too."

I nodded and started gathering my things, along with Bendy's supplies and my original clothes.

Once we finished packing, Bendy, Luca, and I set off on our *final* exploration. We discovered mythical creatures, some of which we even managed to tame. We cooked meals over an open fire, roasted s'mores and marshmallows, and took one last walk through the enchanted forest.

When we returned to the school, we said our goodbyes to the people we had met.

As I placed Bendy on his leash and dressed him in his *famous* costume, the students and teachers waved us off.

"We'll miss you!" they called out.

I smiled and reassured them, "We'll miss you guys, too! But trust me—Luca, Bendy, and I will *definitely* be back. We love this place!"

Then, we spotted the time machine.

With one last glance at our magical school, Luca, Bendy, and I stepped inside.

A few minutes later, we arrived back home.

I gasped. "Oh no!"

Luca turned to me, alarmed. "What? What happened?"

I groaned. "I left my suitcase at the school! I need to go back!"

She sighed, but nodded. "Alright, let's go."

So, with Bendy in tow, we stepped back into the Time Machine.

Within seconds, we were back at Cumberland High School of Magic. Sneaking into our old dorm, I quickly grabbed my luggage. Then, we rushed back to the Time Machine and repeated the teleportation process.

This time, when we arrived home, everything was set.

CHAPTER SEVEN

A Few Years Later
We Go Back

Years had passed, and now I was 20 while Luca Watson was 18. I lived alone with Bendy, and so did Luca—but we lived on the same block, just not in the same house.

One day, after feeding Bendy, my phone rang. It was Luca calling.

"We should go back!" she said excitedly.

I smiled. "Yeah, sure—but only for two hours."

"Aww, no fun—" she started, but I cut her off.

"Well, I *do* have a job, and I'm working the night shift today, so I can't stay for a whole day or anything longer," I explained.

She sighed. "Okay, okay. At least you keep track of your schedule. Let's go!"

With Bendy by our side, we stepped into the Time Machine once again. Except this time... it had been *upgraded*. As soon as we pressed the start button, we were instantly teleported.

When we stepped out, everything felt nostalgic—but also new.

The teachers I had once known were still there, and they greeted us warmly. They petted Bendy and showed us around the school, which had been expanded and improved since we last visited. They even introduced us to their new students, who greeted us just as excitedly.

We spent time exploring the upgraded parts of the school, playing with Bendy, and chatting with the teachers. It was nice to be back, even if only for a little while.

After two hours, I sighed and said, "That was so nice meeting you guys again! Thank you for introducing us to your students, showing us around the school, and welcoming us back. We really appreciate it!"

Luca nodded. "I *totally* agree! I had a great time. I bet Bendy did too! Thank you again—bye!"

The teachers waved us off, and with that, Luca, Bendy, and I headed back home.

After two hours, I sighed and said, "That was so nice meeting you guys again! Thank you for introducing us to your students, showing us around the school, and welcoming us back. We really appreciate it!"

Luca nodded. "I totally agree! I had a great time. I bet Bendy did too! Thank you again—bye!"

The teachers waved us off, and with that, Luca, Bendy, and I headed back home.

Once we arrived, I fed Bendy, and Luca and I decided to have a sleepover—just like old times.

We spent the night watching movies, playing with Bendy, and having pillow fights—laughing until we were too tired to keep our eyes open.

Afterword

I hope you had a great time reading this story. I put a lot of hard work into writing it, and I truly appreciate you for sticking with me!

Acknowledgements

My main help was my mom, so thank you for helping me make this with teamwork. My dad, he kind of helped me with deciding when to stop, and so did my mom, so more credits to her too.

Thanks to my friend who helped me get some of the problems to make the book more interesting! And thank you to whoever read all the book or who bought it!

About the Author

Adrianna is a 10 year old girl who has a huge heart for people and Jesus. She is often found volunteering her time at local community events with her church, is an active basketball player with her school team and still finds time for a little virtual reality fun.

Since the first grade, Adrianna has made straight A's and enjoys school very much.

She enjoys travel (first class when possible) and at the age of 10 has experienced London, Puerto Rico (twice), the Bahamas (twice) and all over the US with both of her parents, Kim & Rich.

Living in an entrepreneurial home, Adrianna truly embraces opportunities like blogging, pinning on Pinterest, writing books and still aspires to become a veterinarian.